HANNAH
and the
Seven Dresses

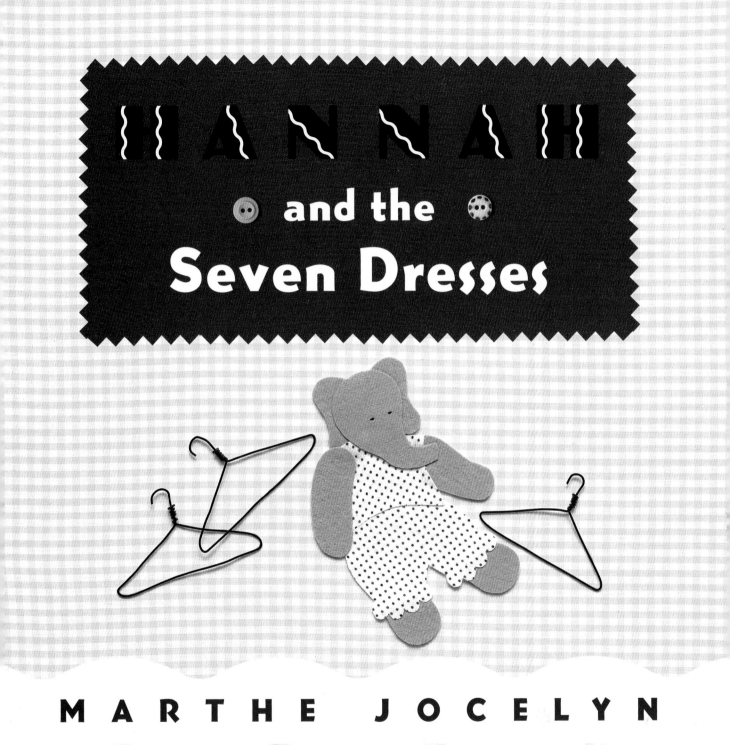

MARTHE JOCELYN

Dutton Children's Books
NEW YORK

FOR TIM

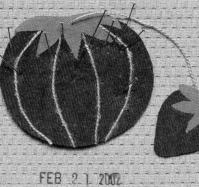

Library of Congress Cataloging-in-Publication Data
Jocelyn, Marthe.
Hannah and the seven dresses/ by Marthe Jocelyn.—1st ed.
p. cm.
Summary: Hannah can never decide which of her beautiful dresses she should wear,
and on her birthday she tries wearing them all at once.
ISBN 0-525-46113-2
[1. Clothing and dress—Fiction. 2. Birthdays—Fiction.] I. Title.
PZ7.J579Han 1999 [E]—dc21 98-19488 CIP AC

Published in the United States 1999 by Dutton Children's Books,
a division of Penguin Putnam Books for Young Readers
345 Hudson Street, New York, New York 10014
http://www.penguinputnam.com/yreaders/index.htm
Designed by Sara Reynolds
Printed in Hong Kong
First Edition
1 3 5 7 9 10 8 6 4 2

Hannah loved to wear dresses. But every morning she had a big problem.

She had a closet full of beautiful dresses because her mother liked to sew.

But when Hannah stood in front of her closet, her face got hot. She shivered all over. Her knees went jiggly and her toes curled under.

It was just too hard to pick which dress to wear.

One Monday morning Hannah pressed her fists against her eyes until she saw fireworks. Then she had an idea that would solve everything!

From then on, every Monday she wore
the red dress with the puffed sleeves
and a bow in the back. That bow was the
most elegant thing Hannah had ever seen.

On Tuesdays she wore the green-checked dress with the deep pockets. She knew they could hold any treasure or insect she might find that day.

On Wednesdays she wore the blue dress covered with scenes from the countryside. She especially liked the deer bounding around the bushes.

On Thursdays she wore the yellow dress with rickrack around the bottom. Maybe it was the rickrack that made the skirt keep twirling until Hannah was dizzy.

On Fridays she wore the gray dress with thirteen buttons down the front. Every button was different, and Hannah knew a story for each of them.

On Saturdays she wore the orange dress with the funny, fat pom-poms all over it. She always had to wear her sunglasses at the same time.

On Sundays she wore the purple dress with a crinoline underneath. She could flounce and bounce all day, even though the crinoline was just a teeny bit scratchy.

Week after week, Hannah wore her seven dresses.

She had no more trouble deciding which dress to wear on Monday, Tuesday, Wednesday, Thursday, Friday, Saturday, or Sunday.

Until her birthday came along.

Hannah's birthday was on a Tuesday. But when she opened her closet and looked at the green-checked dress, she hesitated. Maybe deep pockets weren't the most important thing for a party. Maybe the fancy bow, or the bounding deer, or the twirly skirt, or the pom-poms, or the special buttons, or the crinoline would be better.

As Hannah stood there, her face got hot. She shivered all over. Her knees went jiggly and her toes curled under.

It was too hard to pick!

She pressed her fists against her eyes until she saw fireworks. Suddenly she had an idea that would solve everything!

Hannah would wear all the dresses.
She would wear seven dresses at the
same time!

But by the time Hannah's guests arrived, she was a bit worried. She couldn't tie on her party hat. Seven collars were in the way.

Hannah couldn't play Pin the Tail on the Donkey. Seven pairs of sleeves made her arms too stiff to move!

She couldn't even lean over to blow
out the candles on her cake. Seven skirts
got in the way.

Her face got hot. She shivered all over.
Her knees went jiggly and her toes curled
under.

She was wearing too many dresses.

Hannah went upstairs and stood in front of her closet. She pressed her fists against her eyes until she saw fireworks. Then she had an idea that really would solve everything.

She took off her seven dresses...

...and put on
black pants.
And from that
minute until
now, Hannah
has never worn
a dress again.